The Argument

To Benoît.
V. T.

A very, very big thanks to Arthur, Simon, and Élise
for their valuable help with colors.
V. T.

Published in 2010 by Windmill Books, LLC
303 Park Avenue South Suite # 1280, New York, NY 10010-3657

Adaptations to North American edition © 2010 Windmill Books
Copyright © 2007 Editions Milan, 300 rue Léon Joulin - 31101 Toulouse Cedex 9, France.

CREDITS:
Author: Amélie Sarn
Illustrator: Virgile Trouillot
A concept by Frédéric Puech and Virgile Trouillot based on an idea from Jean de Loriol.
Copyright © PLANETNEMO
Translation by Terry Teague Meyer

Publisher Cataloging in Publication

Sarn, Amélie
The argument. – North American ed. / Amélie Sarn ; illustrations by Virgile Trouillot.
p.   cm. – (Groove High)
Summary: When Lena's brother Yael visits, the Groove Team wonders why Lena and Yael
attend different dance schools.
ISBN 978-1-60754-538-5 (lib.) – ISBN 978-1-60754-539-2 (pbk.)
ISBN 978-1-60754-540-8 (6-pack)
       1. Brothers and sisters—Juvenile fiction   2. Competition (Psychology)—Juve-
nile fiction   3. Dance schools—Juvenile fiction
4. Boarding schools—Juvenile fiction   5. Dancers—Juvenile fiction
[1. Brothers and sisters—Fiction   2. Competition (Psychology)—Fiction
3. Dance schools—Fiction   4. Boarding schools—Fiction   5. Dancers—Fiction]   I.
Trouillot, Virgile   II. Title   III. Series
       [Fic]—dc22

Manufactured in the United States of America

Groove High

Amélie Sarn

The Argument

Illustrations by Virgile Trouillot

Skyview Books

an imprint of
WINDMILL BOOKS™
New York

Me: I'm Zoe. I'm 14 years old, and I'm living my dream: going to Groove High to become a choreographer!

Vic: Vic is my best friend. She's beautiful, blond, and always in high fashion. She is totally fun!

Lena: Lena is too cool. She's an athlete and a rebel. Too bad she can't get herself organized! She always keeps Paco, her chameleon, in her pocket.

Tom: Tom is also super cool. But he's super clumsy. He's got a thing for Vic, who is not interested in him at all.

Ed: Ed likes to seem mysterious and distant. But once you get him going, he's really sweet and a killer dancer!

Yael: Lena's twin brother—but they're nothing alike! He goes to the Kauffman Academy. He's Mr. Fashion and is vain and flirty. But he's got a good heart and is always ready to help his sister.

Kevin: Ed's little brother, the human hurricane. Everywhere he goes, he finds a way to make mischief. But he knows that I love him. His specialty: all kinds of disguises.

Table of Contents

Springtime!

"You see, when I arrived, there was no one there to meet me," Ed says. "I was all alone at the airport in Mexico City, completely clueless."

"Wow, you must have panicked!" Tom exclaims.

Ed shrugs and runs his fingers through his hair.

We're taking a nice walk in the grassy area around the school. We—that's the whole Groove Team: Ed, Tom, Lena, Paco (Lena's chameleon), Vic, and me, Zoe! Ed has been telling us about his latest problems with his mother.

You've probably heard of her: Anna Glovacki, the world-famous ballerina. You may recall she was written up in newspapers around the world when she walked out on the National Opera of Paris right after being named prima ballerina. She's an extraordinary dancer with a very strong personality.

It's my dream to be able to see her dance some day. Right now, she is performing in Mexico.

She and Ed's father divorced years ago and since then she's traveled just about everywhere in the world. Ed hardly ever sees her. Then, on a whim, she sent him plane tickets so he could visit her. But then she was never available while he was there. So all in all, over a three-day period, Ed saw his mother for about 15 minutes max. Naturally, he got sick of that and ended up coming back sooner than expected. He wouldn't ever let it show, but I know he's really hurt.

"One thing's for sure," Lena says, petting Paco, who's sleeping on her arm, "without you, Groove High just isn't the same. We really missed you, Ed!"

I absolutely agree. The sky is a beautiful blue, the air is warm, and the campus seems like a paradise. It's Saturday and most of the students have gone home to visit their families.

"Only one thing wrong," Vic says. "I'm dying to sit on the grass, but I'm afraid I'll get my skirt dirty! I need..."

"You want to sit on the grass?" Tom asks. "Why didn't you say so?"

He takes off his jacket and spreads it on the lawn.

"Your throne awaits you, Princess," he says, giving Vic a little bow.

Vic raises an eyebrow and looks disdainfully at Tom's jacket.

"Are you sure it's clean?" she asks.

Tom's face turns as bright red as some tulips blooming nearby. A perfect match.

"Uh, yes, definitely," he stammers.

Vic sighs and settles herself gracefully on the jacket of her love-sick friend.

"Anyway," she adds, "it's better than nothing."

A smile lights up Tom's face. It doesn't take much to make him happy. He's walking on air because Vic decided to plop down on his jacket! Poor Tom!

I'd like to lie down on the grass too, but after checking my watch, I hold my hand out to Vic to pull her up.

"No time to be lazy. We've got to be in front of the school in less than 15 minutes and ready to go. I definitely don't want to make Khan wait."

Khan is our yoga instructor. Of all our teachers he's the coolest, the most handsome, the greatest, and the nicest, the . . . well, the best! For a weekend outing, he invited students who are not going home to get their in-line skates and go skating in the large city park downtown. After that, we're all having a picnic beside the lake. It's going to be cool!

Vic sighs.

"That's right, I'd forgotten. We'd better get going, especially since I haven't decided what I'm going to wear yet."

Vic is a real fashion diva. According to her, there's a perfect outfit for each hour of the day and for each different activity. She's been known to change clothes three times in two hours.

"And I've got to go back and put Paco in his terrarium," Lena says. "I still haven't taught him how to skate!"

That reminds me of something. "Hey, what about your brother? Does he know how?"

My friend's face lights up. Lena got special permission from Iris Berrens, the school director, to invite her twin brother on this outing. His name is Yael. I've only seen him once, at a school open house, and to tell the truth, he didn't seem all that nice. More like a big phony. But Lena's really excited that he's coming. That's all she talked about this week.

"Don't worry about him! My brother is good at everything!" Lena says confidently.

Then after a moment, she adds, "You girls will be nice to him, right?"

Vic puts her hands on Lena's shoulders.

"Don't worry for a second! Of course we'll be nice to your dear brother," she says. "We'll take good care of him. Actually, I'm really anxious to meet him. Zoe told me that he looks like a male model!"

I start to blush. Vic is really an expert in turning my words around. It's true I told her that Yael was good-looking, but I also said he was not my type!

Not only that, I wonder how he and Lena can even *be* brother and sister. They are complete opposites.

Lena dresses in her own original, offbeat way, but Yael is classic and preppy. You'll see him in white collared shirts, perfectly creased slacks, and leather shoes all shined up. And his hair perfectly styled. Lena is always wearing baggy clothes and some crazy hat!

Just like us, Yael studies at a dance school: the Kauffman Academy. The director of his school is Ed's father.

I know that Ed never even applied to the Kauffman Academy. Of course, he didn't want to be taught by his father. I tried to get in, but . . . I didn't make the cut. For a while, I was miserable over it, but now I'm not sorry at all. I love Groove High!

What I'd like to know is why Lena is not with her brother at Kauffman. If she had auditioned there at the beginning of the school year, Vic and I would have spotted her. And every time I bring up the topic, she changes the subject. I'm really curious . . . that's probably my worst fault . . . but I would never want to make my friend uncomfortable so I don't say anything.

I see that Tom is in a gloomy mood. He comes up to me, frowning, arms crossed. I put my hand on his shoulder and he shoves me away.

"Hey, what's going on?"

"You told Vic that Yael is really good-looking!"

I can barely keep from laughing. My little comment made him jealous!

"Everyone ready?" Khan asks.

Like the rest of us, he has in-line skates and a backpack. You'd almost forget he's a teacher! Yael arrives right on time. His hair is shorter now, but otherwise he looks the same: gray slacks, a white v-neck sweater, a cap, his hair gelled in place, and the latest in-line skates. Khan gives him a warm welcome and says he's delighted to meet him.

Yael replies, "The pleasure is all mine. I've heard excellent things about the instruction you give at this school."

What a teacher's pet! Then he turns to me.

"Hi! It's great to see you again. Your name is Zoe, right? You know, you're as cute as ever!"

I feel like shoving him away. And then I think better of it. After all, a shove is not exactly a sign of welcome!

Now the showoff turns to Vic. "And you . . . you're Vic, of course!"

He steps back a bit, to look at my friend as if he's assessing the value of a painting he's thinking of buying.

"I met you the day of open house. Wow! You're better up close than from far away! You're an absolute knockout!"

Grrrr! He is so full of himself. What arrogance!

Vic raises her eyebrows. "Oh really? Well, unfortunately, I haven't had the pleasure of seeing you far away! But I think I'd like to!"

Ouch!

The smooth-talking Yael is at a loss for words! He definitely wasn't expecting that. After a second, he manages a little laugh, as if Vic has said the funniest thing ever. But it's obvious that he's faking it!

Vic tosses her head, grabs me by the arm, and we walk away.

Khan is standing at the head of our little group. "You haven't forgotten anything?" he asks. "You've got the sandwiches? Good, let's go!"

We're off!

Ed comes up alongside me. On a dance floor, he's as agile and graceful as a leaf blowing in the wind. On skates, it's another story. His knees are turned inward, his head is jerking back and forth, and his arms flap wildly. He seems to be having trouble keeping his balance.

And while trying not to fall down flat on his back, he shows me his camera.

"I'm going to immortalize this outing on film. Maybe we can put the photos in *Groove Zine*."

Hmmm. Considering how shaky he is on his skates, the pictures would probably be totally blurred . . .

I give Ed an encouraging smile. "Great idea!"

He smiles back and . . . grabs my shoulder to keep from falling.

"Hey," he says, looking more serious, "I thought Kim was coming."

Kim! Why is he worrying about that pest?

"Why do you ask? You miss her?" I ask, a little annoyed.

He shrugs.

"It's not that. But you know as well as I do that she never goes home to visit her parents on the weekend. I thought she'd be on the outing. And then, with her ongoing problem . . . "

I shrug too. It's true that the Groove Team was worried about Kim recently. We discovered that she was making herself throw up in order to keep from gaining weight. Usually her brother Luke keeps an

eye on her, but today he's participating in a Brazilian festival. At the same time, I am not at all interested in thinking about the Groove Team's nemesis on such a beautiful day. I listen to what Vic is saying to Lena. On the other side of his sister, Yael skates smoothly along. That guy really gets to me!

"Hey, Lena," Vic says, "there's something I've been wanting to ask you for a long time . . . "

Uh-oh! When Vic's voice sounds all sugary-sweet, it means a disaster is on the way . . .

"Yes, what?" Lena asks, making a perfect half-turn.

No surprise there. Lena is a pro at any sport she tries.

"Why is your brother at Kauffman and you're at Groove High?"

Lena is so taken off guard that she almost falls down. Vic knows as well as I do that Lena always avoids this subject. I wonder if Vic is thinking that with her brother next to her, Lena will have to answer. But Yael has slowed down a bit and now he's behind us. A coincidence?

"Uh, well . . ." Lena starts, skating backward. "I . . ."

She's saved by a pebble, so to speak. An itty-bitty

rock that gets stuck in her wheel. She doesn't have the time to regain her balance and she topples backward, right on top of . . . poor Ed, who takes a big spill this time. Lena lands on him and there they are, all four feet sticking in the air. Tom bursts out laughing and tries to hide it by covering his mouth. He's too nice to make fun of his friends . . . but this is hysterically funny and we all break out laughing! To make up for it, Tom holds out his hand to Lena. I help Ed. They get up, looking very embarrassed. Especially Ed. He's always the neatest dresser, and now he has dirt all over his pants.

Lena dusts herself off. I notice that her brother didn't jump to her rescue. But before Lena has even looked up, Vic charges on. Tact has never been her best quality . . .

"Okay, so why have you two never been at the same school? And, your brother is in second year, right? Since you're twins, you're the same age, so why aren't you . . ."

"Stop!"

Lena's eyes are shooting daggers. Vic stops abruptly. And believe me, it's not easy to make Vic shut up.

"Stop!" Lena repeats. "I don't get why you're asking me all these questions! Anyway, it's none of your business."

Lena takes off in a burst of speed and soon she's way ahead of us. I'm not sure if she's furious or hurt by Vic's nosy questions.

Vic looks at me, acting completely surprised. She

nervously pushes her hair behind her ear.

She acts innocent, like she doesn't understand Lena's reaction, but I know my friend like I know my own name. You know that little gesture, pushing her hair? It tells me she's embarrassed and she knows she went too far.

The problem now is that this has ignited my curiosity like a flame. And my curiosity is much worse than Vic's. It's going to drive me crazy.

I've got to find a way to solve this mystery. Lena has kept quiet about it for far too long.

Yes, It's Definitely Spring!

I have to come up with a better plan. It has to be clever because the way Vic put the pressure on Lena was a complete failure. Let's see . . . What if I just asked Yael? Slyly, of course—I'm good at that. I skate up to him.

"Hey."

He's skating with his hands behind his back. He brushes away a lock of hair that's covering his eye. I say it louder. "Hey."

Finally he turns toward me.

"Hel-LO, cutie! So you finally had enough of hanging around those losers from your school? You're looking for someone interesting to talk to?"

I stare at him, amazed. I don't believe what I'm hearing. What a conceited snob! He thinks he's so cool!

And then he goes on. "Or maybe you're attracted by my natural classiness. I can understand that. I hate to say this, but your friend Tom is kind of a dork. Ed is more sophisticated, like me, but on skates, he's . . ."

Now I'm clenching my fists. If he says one more word, I might . . . ! Just then Lena glides up behind me.

"Hey, I see you two are getting along great!" she says with a big smile. "Neat!"

"You know, Zoe," she says more quietly, with a big warm smile, "I just knew you would appreciate my brother. You're a girl who's really open-minded and the first to accept new people and things. It's what I admire so much about you . . ."

I can feel myself blushing. I unclench my fists. Okay, I guess I can tolerate Yael. I will even try to like him.

Now that I think about it, I can see how Lena feels. She's really happy that her brother is here. From what I can tell, things aren't going so well with their parents right now. Lena hasn't actually talked to me about it, but there were a couple of nights that I've seen her in bed with a letter from one of her parents.

She would read it over and over and cry.

Suddenly, I want to forget everything and just roll along in the warm spring breeze. And it's easy because Khan planned this outing perfectly. Ever since we left the school, we've been skating on smooth, winding paths. People on bicycles are out enjoying themselves, too, and they speed by us. Now we're nearing the river.

I slow down to take a breath and glance back at my friends.

"Is everyone coming?" Khan asks, turning around.

"Right behind you!" Tom says with a wave.

Khan smiles.

Tom hasn't left Vic's side the whole time. Not only that, she gave him her purse to carry. Of course, he took it. He's working harder than usual to attract her attention and make her laugh. But he's out of luck. Vic is only interested in

27

guys a little older than she is. Tom is a year younger, so he doesn't have a chance with her. She does like him—the way you like a pesky little brother. Nothing more. Poor Tom. But I don't really pity him. He looks so happy next to his blond diva. Oh, look, now he's picking some wildflowers growing in an open area . . . not just one or two, a whole bouquet. Just as he's about to stand up and deliver them to Vic, Yael skates right into him and Tom lands splat in the grass.

"Oh, ex-CUSE me!" Yael says and bursts out laughing.

Tom gets up. The knees of his pants are stained green. His flowers are scattered all over the path. Tom bends over to pick them up. Yael just turns away and races off to catch up with me.

"Hey girls, watch this!"

He performs a magnificent jump and lands perfectly on one foot.

Lena claps wildly. "Woo-hoo! Bravo!" she cheers.

Yael grins and bows to her before striding proudly back toward Vic.

On the way, he slaps Tom on the back. "Did you see that, pal? Bet you'd love to be able to do that, wouldn't you?"

Then he skates right past Tom and glides alongside Vic, takes her hand and begins to lead her forward down the path. Tom turns red as a beet (to tell the truth, this is one way Tom and I are exactly alike—we both blush with high-voltage intensity).

I hurry over to him and murmur, "Let it go. He's a real jerk."

Tom has picked up his flowers. The ones that aren't drooping are crushed. He glares at Yael, who

is still holding on to Vic. She shows that she has no desire to skate with him, but he doesn't care. She finally breaks free from him, so Yael pretends he's letting go of her hand. Then he comes over and circles around Tom.

"So you're ready to try that jump? Don't you want to show what you can do? Hey, Vic," he says, calling to her, "don't tell me this guy's your boyfriend? I thought someone with your gorgeous looks could do better than him! You should be going out with someone classier! Someone like me, for example."

I look around for Lena . . . this time she simply has to tell her brother to stop it! But no, I see that she's in back of the group, bending over to adjust one of her skates. The spring day is still warm and but all we feel right now is the icy tension. Ahead of us, Khan hasn't noticed that we've stopped.

Yael continues. "So what do you say, Tom? Ready for a little race? Let's stop at that lamppost up ahead. See it? The one that's a little bent. Right near your teacher."

Tom purses his lips. He glances toward Khan. When Khan told us about the outing, he made it clear that he didn't want to have to watch over us like a bunch of grade school kids. He was counting on us to behave ourselves, to watch out for others, not to skate wildly or go off from the group . . . We all agreed. We gave our word to keep our promise.

"So, you're afraid of looking bad?" Yael says, tapping Tom on the shoulder again.

Tom looks at Vic. She doesn't say anything, doesn't move. He frowns and turns abruptly toward Yael.

"You're on."

"YES!" Yael says, holding up clenched fists as if he has already won.

I shake my head. Guys can be so dumb sometimes. But I know it's useless to try to talk them out of this . . .

"Lena, come here, you're going to have to be our ref!" Yael calls out.

Lena has just caught back up to us. "Ref, why?"

"Tom and I are going to race each other. We're ready. Just give us the signal to start."

Ed is standing off to the side, hands in his pockets. With his hopeless lack of ability to skate, he can't possibly join the race. Besides, he hates this kind of competition. Ed is the type of guy who measures himself only against his personal standards. Lena sends Vic and me a questioning look. Vic's face shows no emotion. I just shrug.

"Okay, then," Lena says. "On your mark, get set . . ."

Yael and Tom are in position, side-by-side, elbows tight against their bodies. Tom still grips the crushed bouquet of wildflowers.

"GO!" Lena shouts.

They're off like a shot. Yael skates well and fast, but Tom is faster. He races harder and begins to take the lead . . . I'm silently cheering him on. When Yael sees that he's about to lose, he grabs Tom's shirt

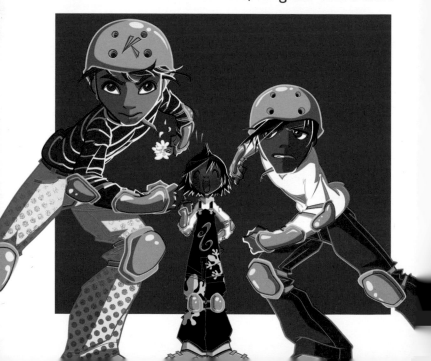

and . . . pushes him!

Then things happen fast. Vic takes off, racing toward the boys. Right after Yael shoves Tom, he completely loses his balance and is about to crash to the ground. Vic arrives just in time. She grabs him and he holds on until he is steady again. Yael races on, but looks back over his shoulder to make sure Tom is not catching up. He never sees a rock coming closer and closer, right in the middle of the path. Yael trips on the rock . . . and falls flat on the ground.

In the end, it's not as bad as it sounds. Yael puts his hands out to break the fall and only scrapes his palms a little.

Now we're all around him, including Khan. He never saw the race at all because he had turned around just in time to see Yael fall.

"Are you all right?" he asks Yael, bending down beside him.

Yael, still on the ground, glares at Tom and Vic. I look over at them too.

Vic has taken the bouquet from Tom's hand and she gives him a little kiss on the cheek.

Are my eyes telling the truth? Now, that is just totally unbelievable!

Chapter 3

Two—No Three!—
Surprise Visits

"**H**ow's this spot?" Khan asks, setting his back-pack on a bench.

It's great. We've stopped in the middle of the park at a grassy area sprinkled with flowers. It's right at the edge of the lake.

Since the end of the embarrassing race (embarrassing—for Yael), he and Lena haven't stopped talking. They talked intensely in hushed voices, but not *that* hushed. You know me, I couldn't help myself, I had to try to listen in. I did hear these few bits of conversation but they only made me more curious.

Lena muttered, "You're just awful, Yael. How could you act like that?"

"Don't preach to me, Lena," Yael replied. "Do I need to remind you what happened two years ago?"

Lena's face fell. Then she said, "That has nothing to

35

do with it. I didn't . . ."

Just then, Ed found me and said he needed me to be in some group photos. Of course, I couldn't exactly tell him I was eavesdropping on Lena and her brother, so I had to go with him.

Now, Vic and Tom are another story! It's like a miracle happened. Vic carefully clipped Tom's flowers to her purse. Then they skated side-by-side in rhythm. Tom was flying on cloud nine. You should have seen him! His feet hardly touched the ground.

But I then I noticed the looks Vic was giving Yael. I'm afraid that all the attention Vic has lavished on Tom was really just her way of trying to put Yael in his place—and it's not a very classy place.

I realize that I'm starving. I can hardly wait to gobble up the tuna sandwich I made in the school kitchen this morning!

We sit down, take off our skates, and put on the shoes we brought in our backpacks. Ed walks over to the lake to take more pictures.

I just can't resist whispering to Vic, "Well, it looks like true love between you and Tom . . . "

She flashes me a horrified look. "Oh, please, you must be kidding!"

Oh, no! Just as I suspected. I decide to push a little more . . .

"Hey, but you took his bouquet and you . . ."

"Stop it!" She cuts me off. "I just thought Yael was acting so stupid back there. I thought I'd teach him a lesson."

I smile knowingly. "Oh really? Well, you're making Tom very happy at the same time."

Just then, Tom, who is discussing something with

Khan, gives Vic a little wave. I poke her with my elbow.

"See! He's more in love than ever!"

Then Tom runs up and drops down on one knee before the girl of his dreams. "Isn't this the greatest day?" he says, smiling from ear to ear.

Vic shakes her head. "Poor sweet Tom," she says. "You're always happy, no matter what."

And then she lies back on her purse, forgetting that Tom's bouquet is there under her head. She crushes it.

It only takes that one motion for Vic to completely squelch all the hope she has built up in Tom's poor heart. (But I'm sure she blushed slightly when I mentioned the bouquet of flowers earlier.) And I know what's behind the role of Ms. Super-Cool that she always plays, and what's behind that confident, I'm-so-sure-of-myself image. Vic has the heart of a true romantic!

Lena and Yael have stopped talking softly. It looks like they're upset with each other. I'd really like to know what they were arguing about a few minutes ago.

What did Yael mean when he asked "do I have to

remind you what happened two years ago"?

I've got to get this straightened out. And to make that happen, I have to get Lena to talk . . . first about something she really cares about.

So I call over to her, "Hey, Lena, did you see that? There's a basketball court over there!"

Lena turns around and cranes her neck to see the backboards.

"A basketball court?" she says. "Why didn't I think to bring a ball? We could have played!"

"Oh yeah?" Vic says sarcastically. "Three against three?"

It's true we don't have enough for a real game. But so what? I'm not serious about playing basketball. I just brought it up to get Lena talking. I continue, "Have you been playing basketball for a long time? You never told us how you got started . . ."

I'll lead her gently down memory lane and end up learning about the mysterious incident two years back . . . I'm sooo clever!

Lena shrugs. "Basketball? I started playing when I was really little. I used to play with my dad and Yael. He's really an excellent player, I . . ."

"Oh, no! It can't be!" Ed suddenly shouts.

He's just come back from beside the lake, camera in hand. He looks like his world has come crashing down. We look in the direction of his gaze.

At the end of the path, we see a familiar figure coming toward us. And just behind it, a much smaller one.

Jeremy and Kevin.

Now I understand why Ed looks so devastated.

Jeremy is the school custodian, who takes care of the building and campus at Groove High. He looks pretty silly with his pant legs clipped tight the way cyclists wear them. There aren't any spokes on

in-line skates to get your pants caught in! To keep his balance, he's holding his arms straight out to each side like a tightrope walker. Even so, he looks like he's about to fall at any moment. I know Ed's not worried that Jeremy is here. Instead it's because . . .

"Zooooooe!" the little blond kid squeals as he jumps in my arms.

"Hi Kevin..."

"What are you doing here?" Ed wants to know. He's already annoyed with his little brother—the most adorable little brat on the planet.

"Daddy dropped me off at your school," shouted his brother, who's dressed as a caterpillar. "He had to leave."

Then he turns to me and announces with pride, "I really scared Jeremy on the way over here! He fell down two times!"

Kevin! I shake my head and roll my eyes.

"Hi, everyone!" Jeremy calls out.

"And hello, Jeremy!" Khan says, getting up to welcome him. "It's nice of you to come and join us!"

"I promised Mr. Kauffman to take the little guy out somewhere. And it's great to be out in this nice weather. Even though Miss Nakamura gave me a lot of paperwork to do. She's always assigning me something new!"

That doesn't surprise me. But . . . where did Kevin go?

"Yikes!"

It's Vic. She shrieking at the top of her lungs and jumping all around. Kevin is right next to her, laughing like crazy.

"She said she's afraid of grasshoppers," he laughs. "So I put one down her T-shirt!"

Oh, no. This can't be happening.

Yael rushes toward Vic. "Wait, I'll help you!" he says with an "at your service" tone of voice.

Of course, Tom wants to be first to rescue his princess. "No, leave it alone! I know how to catch grasshoppers. You shouldn't crush it!"

"Eek! Eek!" Vic squeals over and over like a madwoman. "I can feel it on me! Quick! Doooo something!" She's jumping around and waving her hands frantically.

"I can get it! I can get it!" Tom says as he reaches for Vic's T-shirt.

"No! You can't do that!" Vic is yelling and waving her hands even more as Tom steps right into her way.

Whack! Tom feels a slap and practically sees stars. Vic is still jumping up and down and doesn't notice.

Then a calm voice says, "Here it is. I have the little guy."

It's Lena, gently taking the insect from the knee of Vic's pants and placing it on the ground. Vic lifts her foot to stomp on the tiny creature, but it hops away just in time. Then she spots Kevin.

"You're in trouble!" Vic screeches, running toward

Kevin. "I'm going to get you!"

But Kevin can run much faster than Vic. In less time than it takes to say it, he's off like a rocket.

Tom just stands there, bewildered and dazed, holding his red cheek.

"Just wait till I get him!" Vic roars, taking off after Ed's tricky little brother.

She's so angry that she doesn't see it coming! A collision!

Vic ends up on the ground. Sprawled on the grass across from her . . . is Kim!

I was so absorbed in this whole scene, I never saw Kim arrive. What's she doing here? Did she decide at the last minute to join the picnic?

Physically, Kim and Vic are opposites. Vic, my good friend, is blond. Kim, our mutual enemy, has black hair. Vic's eyes are light blue, and Kim's are dark brown.

"Can't you watch where you're going?" Kim hisses, her voice dripping with acid.

"Oh, dear, I'm so sorry!" Vic snaps, not sounding at all apologetic. "I didn't realize you liked to throw yourself in other people's way. I'm like most normal people. I try to avoid that!"

After I make sure that Vic is okay, I look around for the cause of all this commotion. Of course, the little troublemaker is nowhere to be seen. If I know Kevin, he's probably hiding behind a tree. He'll show up again when things cool down a bit!

Lena takes Vic by the arm and leads her away to calm her down. Ed is listening to Tom, who's still holding his cheek and trying to figure out what's happened. Kim walks across the grass to Khan. She moves like a queen, nose in the air.

"Hello, Kim," he greets her. "So you decided to join us?"

"Hello, sir!" Kim says with her usual phony smile. "I just wanted to finish my homework before coming out. You know how important it is for me to keep up with my studies."

How can she say those words without choking? What a teacher's pet.

Hey, who's jabbing me in the ribs? I turn around . . . it's Yael!

"Who is that beautiful girl?" he breathes in my ear. "Quick, tell me her name! I think I'm in love!"

Chapter 4

Dancing on the Grass

Khan and Jeremy are sitting on a bench talking about relaxation techniques. If I know our yoga instructor, pretty soon he'll have Jeremy trying out some of them! Kim is sitting at the far end of another bench. Obviously royalty like her can't sit on the grass! Only a throne will do. Yael, hands in his pockets, comes up to her. He tosses his head and his long hair flies back.

"Hey, would you mind if I sit here?"

Here he goes. I watch Yael in action.

Miss Snobby doesn't reply.

"Hi," he says a little louder, "may I . . . sit next to you?"

Still no response. Kim doesn't even turn her head to see who's speaking.

Vic, calmer now, is sitting next to me as we take

in this scene. Vic elbows me and we giggle. It looks like this time Yael has really got a challenge on his hands! It'll serve him right to get put in his place, since he thinks he's so great!

He stands casually alongside her, flings back his hair again, and studies his fingernails for a moment (probably hoping his new prey will at least look at him). Nothing. Kim keeps looking straight ahead. We've gotten out our sandwiches. Ed brought a couple of bags of pizza-flavored chips—my favorite! Vic is nibbling on a tomato before turning to Tom.

Raising her eyebrows, she asks. "What exactly is in your sandwich?"

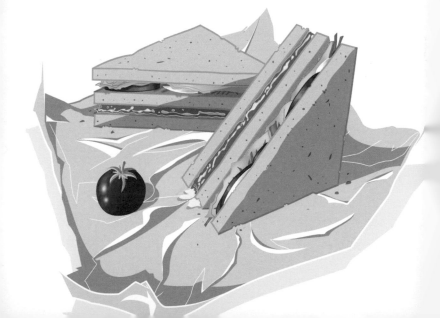

Tom's face lights up. He's so glad his ladylove has forgotten all about the grasshopper fiasco!

"Tuna," he says. "Want some?"

Vic shrugs. "If that's all you've got."

Tom immediately cuts his sandwich in half and gives it to Vic who takes a big bite. Once again, Tom is in heaven. Vic accepted his flowers—yes, I know she squashed them later, but . . . she kissed him on the cheek. Yes, yes—on the same cheek she slapped a little later—well, that was an accident—and now her pearly whites are biting into the sandwich he prepared with his own hands.

Ed has succeeded in corralling his brother and has even gotten Kevin to sit next to him and behave himself. Wow! The kid hasn't caused any commotion for three and a half minutes, so I'm sure another catastrophe is just around the corner.

What's next for me? I'm planning to resume my investigation of Lena. The trouble is—I've got to have a new plan of attack. But, wait! Maybe that won't be necessary. She's leaning over to whisper something to me. Is she ready to confide in me?

"That bugs me," she says.

"What?"

"Watching my brother flirting like crazy with Kim. What does he see in her? It would be so much better if he wanted to go out with one of my friends—you, for example . . ."

Thank goodness he's not interested in me! Should I tell her what I think? Nope! Better to keep it to myself.

Kim sits like a fashion model on the edge of the bench and nibbles daintily on sushi she brought in a little carton. Yael is sitting on the ground, at her feet. Yes, you heard me. His eyes never leave Kim. He just keeps on talking.

"The moment I saw you walking across the lawn, I knew you were different. I sensed that you and I are alike. We're mirrors of each other. And immediately these lines of the great poet Baudelaire came to mind: 'Our two hearts are two vast flaming torches, reflecting their double lights in our two spirits, twin mirrors.'"

Too much! I can't listen to more of this! He's definitely going all out! It looks like he's really got it bad . . . Kim's lips are turned slightly down as if she's rejecting everything Yael says, but the compliments keep pouring out of his mouth. It's getting harder and harder for Kim to resist. Am I seeing things? Kim is blushing! Just a touch of pink, but I can tell! Who would have thought that heartless Kim could blush?

She struggles to keep her aloof attitude as she munches another piece of sushi.

All of a sudden, Yael gets up and holds out his hand to her. Is he going to propose to her or what?

"I have to dance with you!" he declares dramatically.

Mouth full of sushi, Kim is completely astonished. Yael picks up the sushi carton that's balanced on her knees and sets it on the bench. He takes her by her wrists.

How will she react? She's not used to going along with what other people want. Normally, she's giving the orders.

"My sister told me you're working on *Springtime* by Goran Brikovicz. I know that piece by heart. I performed it at my last recital. Shall we try it?"

Kim is just swallowing the last mouthful of sushi and doesn't have time to answer. Yael taps out the beat with his foot and I can immediately hear the music in my head.

Yael dances magnificently. And Kim lets him lead her into the dance. They look really beautiful dancing on the wide green lawn of the park.

Vic gets up and announces, "Say, Groove Team, are we going to let Kim and a student from the Kauffman Academy give us dance lessons? C'mon!"

I look at her and frown. What does she mean?

"Let's go!" she says. "We'll show Yael we know how to dance too!"

Smiling broadly, Ed is already on his feet. You never have to ask him twice to get up and dance. Lena hesitates a moment then gets up too. We line up facing Yael and Kim. They ignore us completely.

"One . . . two . . . one-two-three," Ed counts out the rhythm.

I quickly remove my shoes so I can feel the grass on my bare feet . . . It's great!

Caught up in the movement, I forget all about Yael and Kim, and I just barely notice a little boy disguised as a caterpillar who joins us in a few pirouettes . . .

"Bravo! Bravo!"

Jeremy, Khan, and a small group of passers-by applaud enthusiastically. We were so caught up in our dancing, we didn't even know that we had attracted an audience. We bow before falling down on the grass. The spectators leave, but not before complimenting us again on our performance. We're all feeling fantastic.

"Too bad Mrs. Berrens didn't see that!" Lena exclaims. "She would have been proud of us!"

Yael gives her a big smile. "I must admit that you Groove High students aren't bad!"

Then he leans over to Kim and says softly, "You dance like a goddess. I knew we'd be perfect together."

It's crazy. Even when he's flirting, he's so conceited! But I'm feeling so happy it doesn't bother me. Kim doesn't answer, but I notice she doesn't look as uptight as usual. Who would have thought that one day we'd dance with her without being forced to?

"Wow!" Tom exclaims. "We didn't make a single

mistake and each of us was in perfect time with the others."

"I don't think I've ever danced so well!" Vic declares.

"Zoe had a terrific idea," Khan adds. "I did the same thing she did."

He points to his bare feet. He had taken off his shoes, just as I had. My cheeks turn red. Any compliment from Khan has that effect on me!

Chapter 5

The Game
of the Century

We are all collapsed on the grass, tired and relaxed. I look around.

"Hey, where's Kevin? I wanted to thank him for his contribution to our dance number . . ."

Ed frowns and looks around in all directions.

"Where's he gone now?"

A little worried, I look over toward the lake. With a daredevil like him, anything is possible . . . But there's a whole gang of people over there. If they had seen a little boy fall in the water, they would have surely yelled something . . .

"Over there, on the basketball court!" Lena shouts.

Yes, there he is. He's wandering around a group of boys our age who are practicing passes.

I point him out for Ed. "I'm not so sure they

57

appreciate having your little brother in the middle of their game."

Ed heaves a big sigh and takes off at a run toward the basketball court. I put my shoes back on and follow him. Lena and Tom are right behind us. You never know . . . It's possible that Kevin has already plotted one of his famous tricks and is causing them trouble right now . . .

Yael has gone over to talk to Kim, and Vic is stretched out on the grass. They're not very interested in Kevin.

The biggest player is shouting at Kevin. "Hey, kid, get off the court!"

"But I want to play!" the youngster whines.

"Come back in a few years!" another boy says. "You might get hurt. You're just too little."

"Kevin!" Ed calls out.

Kevin, almost in tears, turns and runs toward his brother. "Ed, they're being so mean! They yelled at me!"

I shake my head. This kid has his own ready-made story for every situation. He bothers other people and then complains that they don't like him. Ed isn't buying his story this time.

"Kevin," he scolds, "I told you to stay with me!"

The other boys aren't paying any attention to us now. They're passing the ball. The tallest one dribbles and takes a long shot that just misses going in the basket.

The other guys slap him on the back and exchange high fives. They quickly go back to practicing.

Lena is at the edge of the court and can't take her eyes off the action. She must be dying to join their game. But she's invisible to the players. They pass to each other, make a couple of baskets, dribble, and slap each other on the back. They're laughing as they practice. Lena is so eager to join them that she crosses her arms, like she's trying to hold herself in—to keep from jumping on the court and into the game. I can tell she's losing her little battle. Now, she can't stop herself any longer. After two or three waves at the players (who completely ignore her), she steps into the middle of the court. The guys continue to act like she's not there. I frown. They really are being kind of mean . . . But Lena doesn't let them get away with it. She intercepts the ball!

"Hey!" one of the players yells. "Who do you think you are?"

"Lena!" she announces proudly, passing him the ball.

"Beat it!" another guy shouts.

Lena is shocked. She didn't expect to be treated this way.

"See, see! I told you!" Kevin exclaims. "They yell at people!"

"First, we get bugged by a little brat and now by a girl!"

The comment stuns me. Maybe for once Kevin wasn't exaggerating. Lena is standing there frozen but I sense that she is about to explode. I know my friend. This could blow up into a real problem.

I remember the old saying "There's strength in numbers." So I turn to Tom. "Go get the others. We might need them."

Tom takes off, running.

Lena's eyes are shooting daggers. "So what's your problem with girls?" she demands.

"We don't want to waste our time!"

"Waste time!" she shouts back. "What do you mean by that?"

Oh my gosh! This situation is heating up even faster than I expected. Luckily, our backup squad turns out to be Yael! Kim apparently didn't feel the need to come to our aid. But I'm not surprised. She's never been inter- ested in us —except to cause trouble.

Yael heads toward the basketball players. "Hi, guys, what's going on?"

"And who are *you*?" the other guy demands.

I shudder. But Yael doesn't back down.

Still smiling, he holds out his hand to the other boy, offering a friendly greeting. "Yael! What's your name?"

The other boy, a little surprised, hesitates for a second. Yael keeps his easy smile as he looks at the boy. The other boy finally shakes his hand.

"Right. I'm Samuel . . . and over there," he adds, pointing to his friends, "that's Stephen, Max, Robin, Arthur, and Alan. We're on a team . . . varsity basketball."

"Sure, that makes sense!" Yael exclaims. "The minute I saw you playing I could tell you're terrific players."

Samuel nods. "Thanks."

Lena's been holding off all this time, but now she bursts out. "I asked them if I could play with them, but they wouldn't let me!" she shouts. "And Yael, the reason they gave is ridiculous. They won't let me play because I'm a girl!"

Lena's accusation changes the mood—suddenly it's less friendly. Ed's mouth drops open and Vic frowns.

Yael glares at Samuel. "Is that true?"

Samuel shrugs. "We don't have any time to waste,"

he mutters again. "We're in training."

"You see!" Lena shrieks, gesturing to her brother. "They think that guys are the only athletes in the world!"

"You're right, Lena!" Kevin's little voice pipes up. "They're a bunch of bullies!"

"Be quiet!" Ed whispers to him.

"Can you believe it?" Lena says, getting more upset all the time. "They think a girl can't compete at their level."

Yael clears his throat. "Relax a little, Lena. Take a breath. You know getting worked up like that won't do any good."

But Lena's not listening to him. Samuel gives her a disdainful look and shrugs. "We told you, we're varsity! We'll be pros some day and you're nothing but . . ."

I don't know what he was about to say, because Tom cuts him off.

"Oh, yeah? You're varsity? The stars of tomorrow? That, I want to see! Are you ready to play us and prove it, or are you scared we'll humiliate you on the court?"

Samuel and his teammates burst out laughing.

Meanwhile, all of us are furious at their attitude.

"Wait a minute," Yael says. "We don't care who wins. All you have to do is let them play with you, that's all!"

I'm totally disgusted. Besides being a phony, Yael is a coward too! He's impossible!

Now Vic, ignoring what Yael just said, jumps in, "Will you make up your minds? Otherwise we might end up thinking you *are* afraid . . ."

Now we all feel the strain of tension in the air. Samuel looks at his teammates. They seem undecided. You can almost see what's going through their minds. They're thinking they have no choice, and if they turn us down, they'll look like wimps who don't have the guts to play against a team that's half girls!

"Okay, okay, we'll play you!" Samuel says. "But once we've demolished you on the court, don't come back crying to us!"

"Go, Groove Team, everyone take your places!" Ed calls.

"Yeah!" Kevin shouts. He's really excited.

"Are you with us or not?" Tom asks Yael.

Yael bites his lip. "You already have five. Six is too

many for basketball . . . "

"They've got six too! If you drop out, they'll have an advantage!"

Yael hesitates a bit longer and then makes up his mind. "Okay!"

New energy is pumping through me like fire. I'm so mad I could scream. These guys think they're stronger than us! They reject Lena just because she's a girl! We are going to teach them a lesson! They are going to be so sorry. Vic, Ed, and I give each other high fives. Then we whoop a loud team cheer!

The others have taken up positions across from us. From the sidelines, Kevin cheers us on.

"Go Zoe! Go Tom! Get out there and win, win, win!"

Yael signals to his sister to position herself at mid-court, ready for action. Samuel is facing her. He can't seem to hide a sneer as he looks her up and down. I'm not surprised since he's a foot taller than she is. But Lena is not intimidated. She looks relaxed and confident.

"Hey," Vic shouts. "Who's going to toss the jump ball?"

We hadn't thought of that! We don't have a referee,

so there's nobody to toss the ball up between Lena and Samuel. We sure can't get the game started without that.

"Me! Me!" Kevin yells, jumping up and down.

I roll my eyes. As if that shrimp could throw the ball high enough! Everyone else just ignores him.

"Stay put!" Yael shouts, taking off at a run.

He races like crazy toward . . . Kim. Still sitting on a bench, she's in her own world, eating her sushi again. She looks up when Yael rushes up to her. I see him talking to her, arms waving. She doesn't move. Is he crazy? Does he think Kim will ever agree to help out the Groove Team? She'd never do that in a million years. I'd expect her to come over and cheer for the other team. But Yael gives her a hug, takes her by the hand, and leads her over to us. She said yes. I can't get over it. Besides, I'm not exactly sure that this is a good thing for us. But we have no choice: no one to toss up the ball means no game. Kim is our only option.

"Unfair!" Stephen protests. "She's with you! She'll give you the advantage!"

Stephen is tall, but not as tall as Samuel. He has very tan skin and incredible blue eyes. He's not as handsome as Luke—far from it—but he's really cute. Okay, where was I . . .

"Ready?"

Lena is totally focused. Knees bent, arms up, fingers spread wide . . . Kim holds the ball in the palm of her hand. Samuel is acting unconcerned. He's so sure he'll be passing the ball to one of his teammates that he doesn't even get in position.

"One, two . . . three!" Kim shouts, tossing the ball in the air.

Lena jumps. Before Samuel has time to react, she smacks the ball as hard as she can. Yael is ready and catches it. He takes off, dribbling straight ahead. We run toward the basket. Yael stops, passes to Ed, who passes to Tom, who passes to Vic, who passes to me. In a flash, Lena is in position under the basket. No one is there to guard her, I throw her the ball and . . . She leaps to make a basket. Swish! YES! Two points for us. The backboard is still shaking. And it's not the only one. Samuel and the others are shaking too— with fury. They can't believe they just let a girl score a basket on them!

They don't waste a second. They've already gotten the ball back. Arthur dribbles. I'm guarding Stephen. We're one-on-one. Lena is guarding Samuel. I can tell that it's a personal rivalry between them. Yael tries to knock the ball away, but he misses. Stephen passes to Alan, who's guarded by Vic. Vic is faster and intercepts the ball, and passes it off to Tom who's at the other end of the court. Tom is already charging toward the basket. But Robin catches up to him and steals the ball away. He passes it to Samuel who speeds toward our basket. We run to defend it. We're all there blocking the basket like a wall, arms held high. But Samuel doesn't even slow down. He rushes toward the basket and shoots it over our heads. He scores!

Awesome! What a fantastic game! I almost feel

like clapping.

Suddenly, I feel a someone nudging me . . . It's Lena grabbing my shoulder to get my attention . . .

"Back in position!" she barks at me. "We can't let them score again!

I know Lena isn't in a bad mood. She's just intense. Lena really wants to win this game!

Chapter 6

A Suspicious Fall

I can't go on. We've been running up and down this basketball court for fifteen minutes without a break. We haven't scored again. Samuel and his team always manage to block us. They are good, really good. Considering that they practice all the time, we're not doing so bad ourselves. Actually, we're doing great. They haven't scored again either. We're giving them a tough battle, and that's really something. After all, we have to remember that they're varsity players. We're just dancers!

I'm so tired, sweaty, and out of breath that I'm ready to call it quits. I wish the other team would think so, too. Haven't we both made our point? They've proved that they are very, very good. We've made them think twice about all their bragging.

After all, they've had to sweat to keep ahead of a team half made up of girls. I'm really proud of that! And, I don't really have to prove a single thing more. I wish I could just go back and lie down on the grass and chat with my friends. But I know Lena. My wishes are definitely not going to come true any time soon! Every minute, Lena becomes more and more intense. She seems to be everywhere at once, guarding Samuel and never letting him have a free shot. At the same time, her eyes are all over the court and she keeps shouting out plays to us. She'll play until she drops or someone drags her off the court!

Vic is red as a tomato and her hair's a mess. She can hardly run anymore. I move toward her and whisper, "Are you okay?"

"Not really," she sighs. "I'm sick of this!"

"VIC! ZOE!" Lena yells at us as she runs by. "Back in position!"

Now, Stephen is blocking me to keep me from receiving the ball. He really doesn't have to work so hard. I don't think I can catch the easiest toss. Ed runs by me and I hear him huffing and puffing. Hey, that worries me a little. Ed has problems with asthma, and the memory of the time we had to rush him to the emergency room is still fresh in my mind.

I try to signal to Tom. It's useless. He's too busy looking at Vic. As for Yael, he was seriously in the game at the beginning—like all of us—but now he seems to be more interested in signaling to Kim on the sidelines than concentrating on his teammates. Actually, Lena is the only one of us who's really motivated. I try to convince myself that we should be a loyal, solid team going for victory. After all, we're the Groove Team. All for one and one for all! Today, it's mainly all for one!

"ZOE!"

I turn my head just at the right moment and . . . the ball bashes right into my nose. I'm dizzy and I can't see straight.

"Hey, pay attention when I pass to you!" Lena yells. Then she takes off to guard Arthur, who retrieved the ball.

Ouch! That really hurts. And instead of asking if I was okay, Lena gets on my case. That's not right! What was I saying before? All for one? I'm beginning to think there's something wrong with this idea . . .

"Tom, stop him!" Lena orders. "Don't let him score!"

But Tom doesn't have the time to react. Arthur is already just below the basket. He only has to aim and . . . he sinks it!

Lena turns toward me. Her eyes are shooting daggers.

"It's your fault, Zoe!" she yells at me. "You're really not into this game anymore. Do you want us to just give up or what? You know these show-offs will just make fun of us if we do."

To tell the truth, at this particular moment, I simply don't care if we win or lose!

"And you, Tom! I've had it with you! You are completely zoned out! At least you could act like you're trying!"

Ranting all the while, Lena still manages to take control of the ball. She makes a dozen fantastic moves as she dribbles down to our opponents' basket. But none of us follow her. Ed is hunched over, hands on his knees, trying to catch his breath. Tom is getting a rubber band out of his pocket and is giving it to Vic so she can put up her hair. (Sometimes Tom likes to wear a ponytail himself, so he always has rubber bands in his pocket.) Vic stares at the rubber band as if it's a half-dead worm and, with a hopeless sigh, takes it.

Meanwhile, Lena is surrounded by Samuel, Alan, Arthur, and Robin. They've got her completely boxed in.

I should run down and help her out of this jam. But her words (and my nose!) still hurt. So, I don't rush to help and I let her fight to get out of this all by herself. It serves her right!

Then my mouth drops open. She is really unbelievable! Somehow she manages to get away from them and she's dribbling to the basket as if her

life depended on it.

Now what's happening? There's a scuffle going on. You'd think it was a hockey match . . . Once again, Lena is trapped by Samuel and his buddies. She struggles, jabs with her elbow, and . . .

Samuel falls. Actually, he's flat on the ground. He's rolling around, holding onto his knee.

We all run over to find out.

"What happened?" Tom asks.

"What happened?" Samuel groans, still holding his leg. "She pushed me, that's what happened!"

Lena, as shaky and pale as I've ever seen her, stares at us. Her eyes are big as saucers.

"But . . . but I . . . " she stammers.

"If you can't tell the difference between basketball and boxing, stay off the court!" Samuel says, in a pitiful voice. "I think maybe you've made me pull a ligament! Do you know what that means to my career?"

Arthur holds out a hand to help Samuel up, but he doesn't take it. His face is contorted with pain.

Kevin comes over and says in his little kid voice, "Oh, Lena, I think you made a booboo."

Lena doesn't even react.

Vic and I are speechless. But not Yael. He has a lot to say.

He grabs his sister by the shoulders and shakes her. "Once wasn't enough, huh? Can't you ever keep yourself in control? He's bigger than you are! Nobody is forcing you to compete against these big guys!"

But what is he talking about?

Lena has tears in her eyes. She shakes her head.

"I . . . I didn't do anything. He fell all by himself!"

"Sure, sure!" Yael shouts. "That's exactly what you said the last time . . . before you broke down and confessed what really happened!"

"But Yael, I'm telling the truth! I'm sure. I didn't do anything. This time, I didn't do anything!"

By now, Lena is sobbing.

"Hey, everybody, maybe we better take care of him," Ed suggests. He points to Samuel, who is still on the ground.

None of his teammates have bent over to check out how hurt Samuel is. So Ed kneels next to Samuel, who's holding his knee with both hands.

"Let me see," Ed says quietly.

Samuel shakes his head and moans. "No, it hurts too much."

"Maybe we should call for an ambulance," Tom suggests nervously.

I look at Lena. She hasn't stopped sobbing. I've never seen her so upset and miserable! But I can't keep myself from thinking that this was going to happen sooner or later. One side of Lena is my adorable good friend who wouldn't hurt a fly—in everyday situations. But when she's in a sports competition, her athletic drive makes her pushy—no, it's more—she gets extremely aggressive. Take this game. It's a perfect example. She got overly excited and she couldn't control herself. She wanted so badly to win. She just got carried away. Part of me wants to give her a hug, make her feel better, and tell her it's all going to be okay. Another part of me is angry. I can still hear her fierce commands ringing in my ears.

Kim has walked over to join the group. She looks Samuel up and down and shows no concern at all.

"I'll bet there's nothing wrong with him!" she announces. "I saw him fall. How could he hurt himself from a little fall like that?"

But no one is listening to her.

Yael turns toward his sister, his face twisted with anger. "Just own up to what you did right now! You'd better find your teacher and tell him what happened."

Lena does what he says. Her head is down as she hurries away. She hears Yael call after her, "And don't be surprised if you get kicked out of school again!"

Truce

Samuel refuses to move. He maintains that his knee is shattered in a thousand pieces and that he'll never be able to play basketball for the rest of his life.

I'm beginning to wonder if Kim is right for once. Isn't Samuel overdoing it a bit? It's odd that his teammates don't seem very concerned.

"This is what happens when you play with beginners," Samuel says in a pained voice. "And it's even worse with girls! When she realized your team didn't have a chance, she cheated!"

I'm turning a question over in my mind. What was Yael referring to a few minutes ago? Why did he ask if once wasn't enough for her?

"Now what's going on here?"

Khan is here, accompanied by Jeremy. Lena is

following them. She doesn't lift her head to meet our eyes.

"It's that girl!" Samuel exclaims. "She pushed me! She should know that rough contact isn't allowed in basketball! Because of her, I'm going to miss the playoffs. She's probably wrecked my whole life!"

He is definitely making a big deal out of this. And I've just decided that this guy is acting like a jerk. In two steps, I'm at Lena's side. I put my arms around her shoulders. I don't care about how she talked to me during the game! I can't stay mad at her just because she was so intense during the game. That's nothing, when I think of all the things that we've done together, all the times she's supported me, all the times she was at my side when I needed her!

I look at Khan. In a firm, steady voice, I make my statement. "We don't know exactly what happened. No one was really watching and, all of a sudden, we heard Samuel yell and saw him on the ground!"

Lena raises her head and looks at me with surprise.

I don't know if what I am doing is the right thing. I'm defending Lena just because she's my friend, even though I am almost certain she pushed

Samuel . . .

"She pushed me!" Samuel howls. "She couldn't stand losing the game!"

Khan kneels down next to him. Ed moves aside to make room for him.

"Let me have a look at it," our teacher says in a calm voice.

"No!" Samuel protests. "I want you to call an ambulance. They've got to take me home! My parents are going to sue that girl, and your school too! My friends are witnesses . . ."

Khan raises his eyebrows and looks over at Samuel's teammates. Strangely, all of them look away.

I squeeze Lena's hand.

Vic comes over to us. So does Tom. "It's true. None of us saw Lena push Samuel," Vic says.

"He could have easily fallen on his own," Tom adds.

"Or maybe Alan or Arthur bumped into him," Ed suggests.

"Yeah! That could be it!" Kevin shouts with his little know-it-all voice.

I let go of Lena's hand to grab Kevin by the shoulders. I clamp my hand over his mouth to make him be quiet. We don't need him make any more trouble for us!

Lena's tears have stopped. Now, she looks straight at each of us, her mouth half-open.

Khan looks down and, with his usual cool, takes Samuel's calf, and presses on it gently. Samuel cries out as if he's being tortured.

"Alan, Arthur, Robin, tell him to let me go!"

"Take it easy, now, and don't move," Khan instructs him.

But Samuel won't listen. He struggles, tries to push Khan away, and . . . gives Khan a big kick with his left leg. The very leg he couldn't move a second ago!

"Oh, that's fine," Khan says. "It looks like you're much better . . ."

Samuel holds completely still, his faces slowly turning red. Khan takes the injured knee in his hands and begins to massage it firmly.

"Excellent, young man," he says. "I can assure you that your ligaments are intact. You don't even appear to have a sprain! I think you can probably stand up!"

Samuel remains motionless. Khan stands up and holds out his hand. After a moment, Samuel takes

Khan's hand and stands up. He's not even grimacing. There was nothing wrong with him.

"I'm confident," Khan says, "that you'll be able to make the playoffs and your life is not ruined! You can even continue this game! I'll be happy to act as referee."

Khan's eyes are bright with mischief. I can tell that he's making fun of Samuel.

"Unless," Khan continues, "you already have a ref?"

"I am the referee! It's me!" Kim announces.

"Kim!" Khan exclaims brightly. "Well then, perhaps you can shed some light on this incident!"

"Well . . ."

Kim hesitates. What did she see? What is she going to say? Will she take advantage of the situation, as always, to make trouble for a member of the Groove Team?

I let go of Kevin. I think he got the message. I take Lena's hand again, showing I'm her loyal Groove Team friend.

Kim looks at us, one by one. I can tell she is really enjoying this moment. We are in suspense, hanging on every word she says.

"To tell the truth," she starts out slowly, "I . . . I didn't see it all that well . . . Of course, we all know what Lena is like . . ."

I shake my head slightly.

"We know that she's capable of doing the very worst," Kim goes on, "and once again . . ."

Yael's eyes never leave Kim's face. I'm surprised, though. Kim seems troubled . . .

"Yes, Kim, go on," Khan says.

"Well," Kim says, hesitatingly. "I . . . there was a

sort of scuffle around Lena. All of Samuel's team was blocking her at the same time and suddenly . . . Samuel fell and started yelling."

Unbelievable! A look from Yael and Kim changed her mind! We all noticed it! Khan smiles.

"Very good. We have Samuel's version, and now a version from Kim, who was the referee. Now let's hear from Lena . . ."

My friend bites her lip before beginning to speak.

"I . . . I was very hyped up and I could see that we were going to lose," she says softly. "I didn't want that to happen. Samuel made me mad when he refused to let me play just because I'm a girl, so I wanted to teach him a lesson . . ."

"You see!" Samuel shouts. "She admits it. This girl is trouble! She's lucky I'm not injured! And even though I'm okay, all the same, I can tell you she's going . . ."

Khan interrupts Samuel with perfect composure. "Please continue, Lena."

"So, well, I was upset, it's true. And I was mad at the others because they didn't care as much about winning as I did. But when Samuel's team ganged up on me, I realized there was nothing I could do. Samuel was trying to take the ball out of my hands . . ."

"What a liar!" Samuel cries out.

"But I just couldn't let him. I yanked on the ball and that's when Samuel threw himself on the ground and started screaming."

Khan doesn't say anything. He's no longer smiling. Obviously, one of the two is lying. Samuel or Lena? That's the question.

"If you'll permit me," Jeremy says suddenly, "I will stand behind the reputations of Lena and her friends. Sometimes they make mistakes, but they're all basically good and . . ."

"You are right, Jeremy," Khan says. "They are all good at heart . . ."

What a guy, that Jeremy! He didn't see any of the game, but he's standing up for us just the same! Maybe we should make him an honorary member of the Groove Team.

"They're all basically good," Khan repeats, "but as you say, they also make mistakes from time to time . . ."

Oh no! It can't be true! Khan thinks that Lena is lying! He thinks we're all lying! It's terrible! Khan is my favorite teacher and I would hate if he ever thought badly of me!

"Everyone makes mistakes," he goes on, his tone softening. "I wasn't here to witness the incident, but at least two people here know the truth: Lena and Samuel. It's up to them to reflect on what they did and what they said about it! It's up to them to make peace with their consciences."

Having said this, our teacher heads slowly back to the bench. Jeremy watches him leave and then asks us, "Do you need me?"

I shake my head. "No. It'll be all right. But anyway, I think the game is definitely over."

Jeremy nods.

"Good. Then I'll go back. I was really enjoying my

conversation with Khan. He's such an interesting person. And you know? He's right. You know? What he said about letting your conscience guide you?"

I smile at him. Jeremy is really a great guy.

"But," he adds softly, addressing Lena, "I just want you to know that I'm confident in you. I'm sure you told the truth!"

Yes, he definitely deserves a place as honorary member of the Groove Team!

Jeremy has barely walked away when Samuel bursts out laughing and does high fives with his teammates.

"Okay then, GIRLS!" he says sarcastically. "Do you forfeit the game?"

"I thought you couldn't play," Vic replies. "Remember your terrible so-called injury?"

"Well I guess I'm all better now!" Samuel says. "Now we can . . ."

But he doesn't finish his sentence. Yael leaps forward and grabs him by the collar.

"You were faking this whole time! You wanted to get my sister in trouble!"

"Hey, hey, let me go!" Samuel whines, trying to get loose.

"He's right, Yael. Let him go!"

It's Lena. She jumps between her brother and Samuel. Maybe she wants to take care of him herself! Oh, boy! I wouldn't want to be in Samuel's place!

Chapter

8

Promises to Meet Again

"Let him go," Lena insists. "This guy is not worth getting into trouble."

Yael releases him, and Samuel rubs his neck, but this time, he decides not to make a big deal out of any problem.

"Hey, let's go," Lena suggests, turning away from the basketball court. "I'd really like to go back and sit on the grass."

What a wonderful idea! Without looking back at Samuel and his teammates, we head back to the grass. Everyone follows, even Kim.

Vic, Tom, and I surround Lena. Ed goes off to get his little brother who's jumping around in the grass. Terrific! For once he's not plotting one of his crazy pranks!

Yael is a little behind us, deep in conversation with Kim.

As for me, one question is driving me crazy.

"Say, Lena . . ."

"What?"

"What was your brother talking about a while ago? You know, when he said . . ."

It's harder than I thought. I can't even look Lena in the eye.

"When he said I might get expelled from Groove High . . . that's what you want to know?"

I shrug. I have the feeling that I'm about to find out the answers to all those questions I've been asking Lena for so long . . .

"Here goes," Lena says, very quietly. "Two years ago, Yael and I were at the same dance school. We were even in the same class. There was a girl there who really bugged us."

"Really? What did she do?"

"She'd make fun of us and treat us like . . ."

"Like what?"

"Like spoiled rich kids."

I'm thinking back to the day of the school open house in October. It was a big surprise to me. Lena is a really cool girl—so natural. She's not at all stuck up. When her parents came, she put on a pleated skirt and a preppy white blouse. That style is the complete opposite of her usual outfits. She always dresses in her own original way. Her accessories are a cap or bandana or big wacky earrings. Then I met her parents. I realized that they were very fashionable and sophisticated types. I felt they were the kind who think of themselves as so classy they don't mix with just anybody.

"You see," Lena continues, "my parents had a chauffeur who drove us to school in a limo every morning. They made me wear clothes that I hate and never stopped trying to run my life. One time, they made a fuss at school because some third-year students threw a big party over the weekend! And I didn't even go to the party!"

Now I get it! It must be tough to have parents like that! And I think my mother is a pain!

"They don't say anything about Groove High because I don't give them a chance to," Lena says, a little sadly. "They're not very happy with it, though. They think this school isn't good enough for any member of the Robertson family."

Another memory flashes in my mind. It's what Mrs. Robertson called her daughter at that school open house that we'll never forget . . .

"*Helena*. Is that your real name?"

"Yes," Lena answers. "But I don't allow them to call me by that name!"

I agree. For me, Lena is Lena. Now I really want to know the rest of the story.

"So what happened with the girl who was always bothering you?"

"During PE class, we were arguing over a basketball game. She was guarding me and just wouldn't stop making fun of me under her breath. At first, it didn't bother me. I just ignored it. But then . . . she pretended to fall. The referee wasn't looking at us. The girl said that I had pushed her and her team should get a free throw. The ref agreed. I was so furious I could hardly stand it. She made the point. Back in the locker room, she kept on taunting me and I don't know what came over me. I grabbed her by the arm, I shoved her against a wall and . . . and . . ."

"And what?"

I can't get over it.

"She got hurt . . ."

"Yes," she said. "Exactly. Of course, she reported me to the principal and the dean. In the end, I . . . I got expelled."

At last! Now I understand everything. Well, not everything yet.

"The sad part is that I probably would have gotten off with just a punishment if I hadn't lied. From the beginning I told everyone I had never touched that girl. I denied the whole thing. I kept saying I hadn't touched her. That's why Yael wouldn't believe me back there. But this time, I'm telling the truth. I didn't do anything to Samuel. He was irritating me, for sure. But I tell you, I didn't touch him. I would never do that to anyone again."

I smile at my friend.

"Don't worry, Lena. I believe you."

"I also wanted . . . to thank you," Lena said. "And to apologize. I realize now I was just awful to you during the game. I kept yelling and saying you weren't trying . . . and you were there for me when I needed you, Zoe. You were the first to stand up for me."

What a friend!

"I'm sure you would have done the same thing for any of us. After all, we're the Groove Team, right? One for all and all for one!"

A beautiful afternoon in early April. Green grass, a glassy lake, friends just hanging out and talking. What more could you want?

Lena has told her story to Ed, Vic, and Tom. They all offered their support and unconditional friendship. She also went to talk with her brother. We saw them hugging each other!

After that, Lena came back to our group and Yael went over to Kim, a little away from everyone else. The two of them have been together all afternoon. Interesting, huh?

Khan finally got Jeremy to try some yoga, and he really liked it!

Khan is a fantastic teacher. I suspect Samuel's act didn't fool him for a second.

Oh, that reminds me. Samuel and his buddies! From where we are sitting, we watch them start to practice again—until Samuel smashes into Arthur like a truck. The poor guy falls and seems to be hurt. He finally gets up, but that ends their game. The six of them leave, with Arthur limping slightly. But what do you expect? When you can't tell the difference between boxing and basketball, stay off the court!

Just as we are talking about the next issue of the *Groove Zine*, a big black cloud covers the sky and it starts raining cats and dogs. We barely have time to gather our things and hide under a bus shelter.

Now it's time for Yael to leave.

When a crowd of people huddle close together in a bus shelter, it's not so easy to have a private conversation. Yael and Kim try to talk softly, but we can't help hearing them. They exchange telephone numbers and e-mail addresses and promise to see

each other again as soon as possible. Then Yael races off, hunched over to protect himself from the rain. It's not so easy to ignore another thing. It's Kim's long, lingering gaze at him as he disappears.

And one last thing. You can't help noticing her big smile when he turns back to give her a last wave.

We are totally soaked when we get back to school.

Everyone changes and meets back in the cafeteria for hot chocolate. Kevin is perfectly happy. He manages to spill it all over the place.

Out of the big cafeteria window, we watch the rain falling on the green campus lawn.

This was the most fantastic April day!

Three cheers for spring!

GROOVE Zine

Edited by the Groove Team

One for all...

I know, I know we are in a dance school. Still, if we have sports in our program, we should try to be our best at them! We have much to learn about playing together and, above all, team spirit. In life, it's about helping others, but also about getting help! We must be willing to look around us for the things we can't do ourselves. United we are stronger, and we must never forget that.

So the Groove Team gives you a tip: Take care of your friends!

Yael Robertson—A Deeper Look

Groove High had the honor of a friendly visit from Yael Robertson, the brother of Lena Robertson, and a student from another dance high school, the Kauffmann Academy.

GZ Yael, are there many differences between your school and Groove High?

YR I think we have more hours of dancing at the Kauffmann Academy. It is a school that emphasizes technique.

GZ And what about the atmosphere?

YR: The atmosphere is very different from the Kauffmann Academy. We are not as close to our teachers as you are here.

GZ: You are thinking perhaps of Khan, our yoga teacher?

YR Yes, he is truly extraordinary. In fact, yoga is not taught at the Kauffmann Academy at all.

GZ And do you have a webzine like our Groove Zine?

YR At Kauffmann, we are more individualistic. The competition is fierce. Which is a shame ...

GZ Thank you, Yael. Finally, do you want to send a message to the students of Groove High?

YR Yes, of course. I loved your school. You made me feel welcome and I really appreciated that ... and I would like to add a special thought for one of your talented students who will know who I am talking about.

GZ Thank you, Yael, good luck to you and we hope to have another meeting between our two schools soon!

School News

by Zoe

Latest Trends

Spring is Here!

Yes! You've all felt the sweetness in the air ... spring is coming. And with spring, I'm sure you're wanting to renew your look! But do not worry, the novelty you want does not necessarily mean emptying your wallet. Here are some tips:

1) Hair—a trim to refresh your cut will be welcome. Just a trim can make you feel like you have a new style.
2) Earrings—you certainly have old beaded bracelets laying around. Have fun and recycle them by mounting them on earrings. This creates a cool effect. Choose beads shaped like fruits and flowers for Spring.
3) Clothing— in April, you'll want to celebrate being able to say good-bye to heavy coats, but don't get ahead of yourselves. To avoid getting colds, match a light spring top with a jacket or scarf.
4) One last tip—sew small fabric flowers on jacket to give it a new look!

by Vic

Sports Page

Don't Confuse Basketball with Boxing

This month, I'm talking about basketball. This is an extraordinary sport in many ways. First, it is a sport where it is impossible to play alone. While a player can dribble the entire length of the court or make a long-distance basket, that's not usually the way the game is played. The key is to work as a team. Players should almost always have an eye on their teammates and be ready to pass or catch the ball. And it's important to remember that the rules of the court are different than the rules of the boxing ring. No throwing punches! Keep your hands to yourself and your eye on the ball.

by Lena

Music Corner

Spring Gives Us Wings

For those who can't get along with the songs of birds alone, remember these invigorating music genres:

1) Enjoy some hip hop.
2) Good old rock. Maybe check out the group BlueDay—even their name sounds like a tribute to spring.
3) And don't forget a bit of classical music—Vivaldi's Spring!

★ ★ ★

by Tom

CINEMA

Romantic Comedies

Spring is the season of hay fever but also of love, so let's focus on romantic comedies:
- Check out Cinderella Story, a light and funny film that will leave you dreaming.
- Maybe try a love story with a bittersweet ending and get ready to be a shoulder to cry on for your sweetheart or let your sweetheart see your softer side.
- And finally, because Groove High is a dance school!, don't miss Diary of a Future Star, you will both laugh and cry!

by Ed

HOROSCOPE

by Zoe

Aries
Spring may cause your head to turn at something surprising. Let yourself be carried away!

Taurus
For once, you feel perfectly in synch with the group. Enjoy it and remember to stay flexible.

Gemini
At this moment, you are anxious and you do not understand why. Maybe it's the change of season? Don't worry, your mood will improve soon.

Cancer
Are you still making complicated plans to get your way? Let things happen on their own for once!

Leo
You have dark circles under your eyes. You should sleep better!

Virgo
Bravo, this week, your sense of justice outweighed your bad thoughts! Keep it up.

Libra
The boy or girl you have a crush on? Do not despair, it is only a matter of time.

Scorpio
It looks like your stars are favorable. You just need to lighten up to enjoy them a little more.

Sagittarius
Once again, you have been carried away by your passionate nature. Try to turn this sometimes over-the-top enthusiasm into a positive quality!

Capricorn
Much imagination and creativity are on the horizon for you this week. Free your mind up to enjoy them.

Aquarius
Stop beating around the bush. The arrival of Spring gives you wings, so fly!

Pisces
You feel that you are a poor lonely person who will never meet their soulmate. Have some patience, there's someone out there for you!

Our School

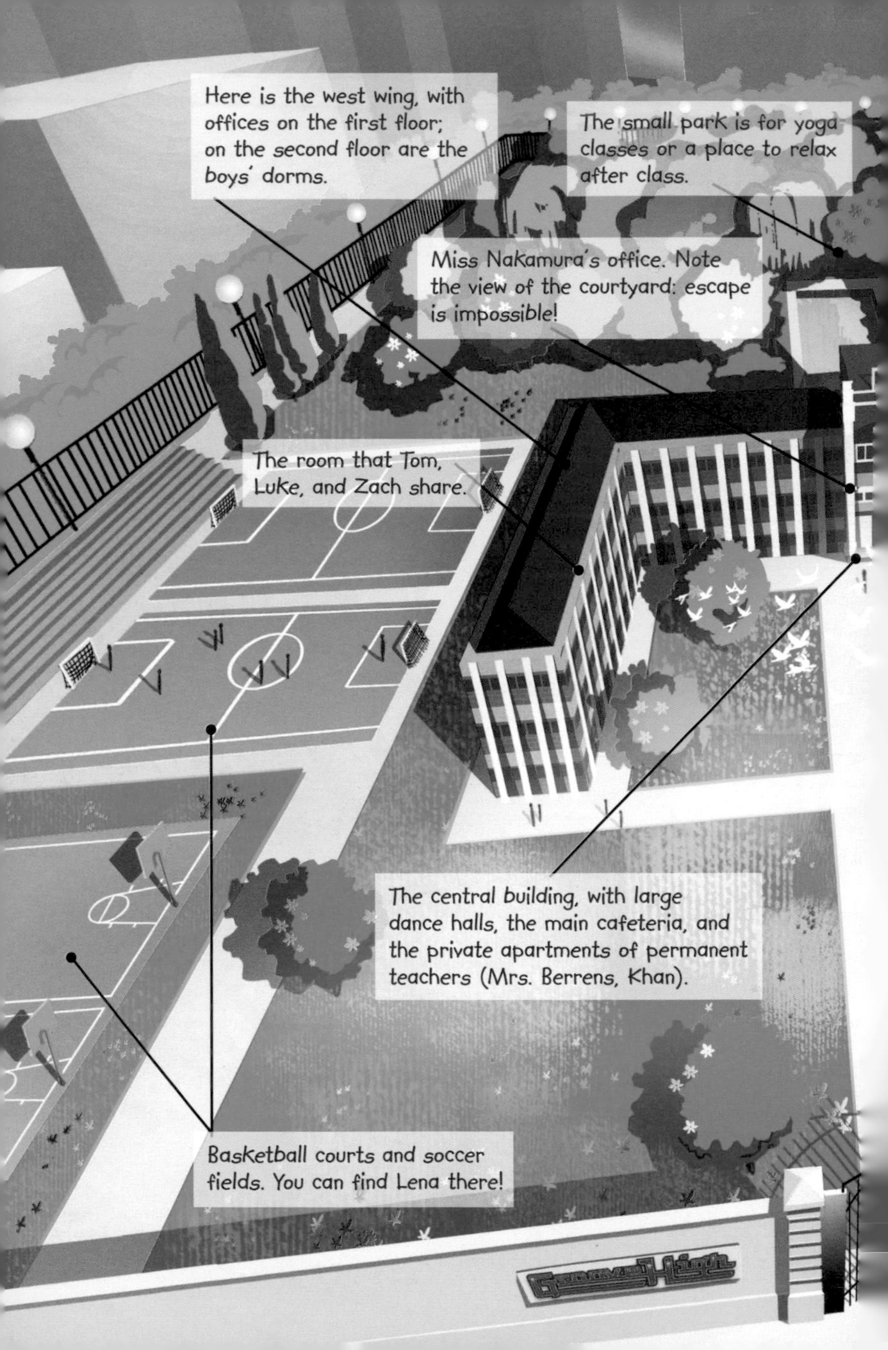
Here is the west wing, with offices on the first floor; on the second floor are the boys' dorms.
The small park is for yoga classes or a place to relax after class.
Miss Nakamura's office. Note the view of the courtyard: escape is impossible!
The room that Tom, Luke, and Zach share.
The central building, with large dance halls, the main cafeteria, and the private apartments of permanent teachers (Mrs. Berrens, Khan).
Basketball courts and soccer fields. You can find Lena there!

Our Dorm Room

Fashionably designed, well-lit, and well thought-out! Here's a small tour of the room . . .

Here is Vic's closet. On the inside, you enter the fashion dimension.

My closet. Vic stores her extra clothes here.

Vic's bed is always neatly made . . . and Paco loves to hide there.

Photo of my cat, "Nama."

Vic loves Lena, her favorite singer.

My bed.

Vic's dirty little secret—her collection of romance novels.

Vic's desk. Just don't leave fingerprints.

You can't see my desk from here, but it's the same as my roommates'. Past the staircase is the doorway out.

Here are Lena's bed and desk (you can't tell how messy her desk really is from this picture!)

Lena's closet is tucked in here by mine. Vic doesn't keep her clothes in here because of the dead bugs Lena keeps inside.

Here's a view of the lower level of our room, under the loft.

The door. Only Tom doesn't quite understand that you're supposed to knock before you come in.

My beloved heater. I love him so much, I even gave him a name: Raymond. (Don't ask me where that name came from.)

Here's my desk, which you couldn't see before. It is strategically placed near the heater, because I'm like Paco — always cold!

We each have our own sink in the bathroom, which makes it easy to get ready together. Vic has a tendency to invade my territory and Lena's.

Very practical: Our bookshelves are built right into the walls.

The bathroom, where we hide Paco's terrarium when we're in class, under the sinks and behind the clothes hamper. (We move that hamper often, between Lena, who always goes out, and Vic, who changes clothes three times a day!)

When we're in the room, Lena keeps Paco's terrarium on her desk.

The boys' dorm room

The exact same layout as the girls', just with different colors.
Personally, I like their room better. What do you think?

Because Tom's closet is far from full (I never understand how boys get by with so little clothing), Vic convinced him to let her keep her "out of season" clothes and shoes in there.

Tom has two treasures: his poster of Vic, and the toy duck he takes in the bath. But Shhh! No one knows.

Luke's corner. He's a die-hard capoeira fan, as you can see from his posters.

Tom's corner. A miracle of housekeeping, according to him. He also makes everyone's beds and keeps the room tidy.

Zach's corner. In his closet he has an impressive collection of basketball uniforms, all from famous professionals.

Tom and Luke switched desks because Luke doesn't like to be so close to the heater. This boy and I are complete opposites.

Poster of Fernando Yace, the most famous capoeira dancer right now. He is supposed to come to Groove High at the end of the year, and Luke talks about him constantly.

Tom is not a big reader, but check out his awesome music collection!

The bathroom: same as ours. "Wow, for a boys' bathroom, it's pretty clean," Vic says.

Luke's desk. It's in the same place as Vic's, which fills her with joy. She sees it as a sign...

Zach's desk. He's a nature-lover. He takes good care of his plants.

Speaking of hiding places, under the boys' sink are stereo speakers, juice, and snacks for a little party now and then.

About the Author and Illustrator

Amélie Sarn: Amélie has two major flaws: excessive curiosity and a tendency to gorge herself. Not just on food, but on reading, travel, games, children, friends, and anything that makes her laugh. This gives her lots of material for stories! When her publisher asked her to write the stories of Zoe and the Groove Team, she revealed her dark side. Of all the characters in *Groove High*, she admits that her favorite is Kim!

Virgile Trouillot: With his feet on the ground, but his head forever in the clouds, Virgile spent his youth under the constant influence of cartoons, manga, and other comics.

When he's not illustrating *Groove High* Books, Virgile develops animated series for *Planet Nemo*. Virgile spends time in his own version of a city zoo that's right in his apartment. His non-human companions include an army of ninja chinchillas that he has raised himself and many insects that science has not yet identified.

Web Sites

In order to ensure the safety and currency of recommended Internet links, Windmill maintains and updates an online list of sites. To access links to learn more about the *Groove High* characters and their adventures, please go to www.windmillbooks.com/weblinks and select this book's title.

For more great fiction and nonfiction, go to www.windmillbooks.com.